AF484950
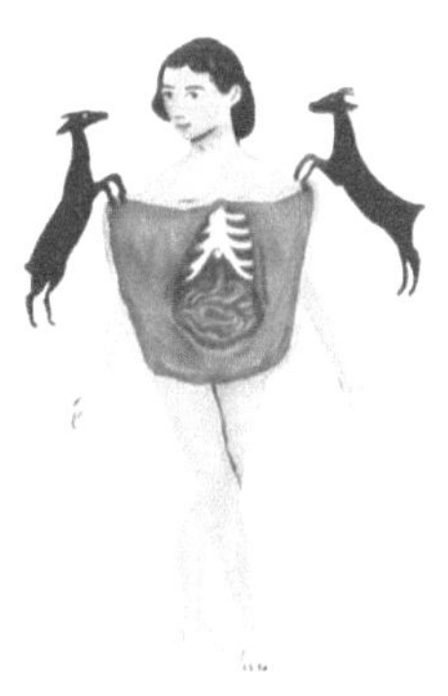

Carlota Roby

Lilith

TIN
TA
PU
JO

Lilith

Lilith

For A.
as always.

Who else
would so envy the bond we had then
as to tell us it was not earth
but heaven we were losing?
Louise Glück, Vespers

I am a woman
and that is all
that matters now

In the ancient legends of Mesopotamia and the Jewish tradition, Lilith emerges as Adam's first companion. Unlike Eve, who was formed from one of Adam's ribs, Lilith was created from the same earth as Adam, sharing equal origin and autonomy. In astrology, Lilith symbolizes the power of feminine energy, dark and wild, present in all living things. Lilith reveals the truth behind our desires and impulses, especially those we dare not acknowledge. In her firm resolve not to be subjugated by anyone, Lilith was expelled from Eden. But who would desire an Eden if it only meant servitude?

Lilith

Chankiri

"I flee and cling to all those windows
Where one can turn one's back on life."
Stéphane Mallarmé

In an empty village
there are carousels full of
withered flowers.
The dry petals crackle under
the weight of
small beasts that approach
to sniff the rusted machines.
There, my childhood remained
full of atomic bombs that
never exploded,
and bordering it,
a path of stones that
sounds like childhood,
something like hearing my parents' car
over the gravel.
Now only the petals are heard,
crackling under the weight of those beasts
that hold as much anger as I do.
We are all radioactive beings
full of resentments
with mines lodged
in our chests.

Carlota Roby

La ciénaga

In la ciénaga, I see my father
feeding fish that are destined to die
when winter arrives.
He raises his right arm and
wipes the sweat from his forehead.
His bare feet anchored
to a rock
while I watch him from a
boat
that I've built from fallen tree trunks.

Father,
sometimes I think of you in la ciénaga
and I want to believe that you're sheltering me
from the cold.
Sometimes, I search for some reflection of you
in the mirror:
> **and I don't find it**
> I search for the umbilical cord:
> and I don't find it,

Lilith

I search for a cell:
and I don't find it,
I search for you making love
with strangers:
and I don't find you.
Father,
sometimes I want to kill you
when the beasts arrive:
and I don't find you.

Carlota Roby

Stray Dogs

I remember your arms outstretched
between the water and the mud
when I was drowning
in la ciénaga,
and I told you
that my only fear of dying
was the immateriality of spirits.
I felt a tremor in your hands
of great dimensions,
and I knew you were crying.
The veins in your hands
looked like the roots
of a very tall tree.
From then on began the
habitual vacillations
of my future self.
I refuse to list them
for there are certain corners
that refuse the looting
of honesty.
I only allow
some prerogatives,
from anger
to poetry.

Lilith

A fly buzzing in my ears

On the grass grew little yellow flowers,
and sometimes as I lay down
and closed my eyes to see them,
a universe appeared
of small and large things;
ants in formation
carrying crumbs of bread,
worms peeking their
tiny heads from the soil,
colorful ladybugs bringing
good luck on their wings,
laughter that seemed so distant,
my grandmother's big lunches
and her short legs dangling from
the chair,
and sometimes, a fly buzzing in my
ears
as I drifted off to sleep.

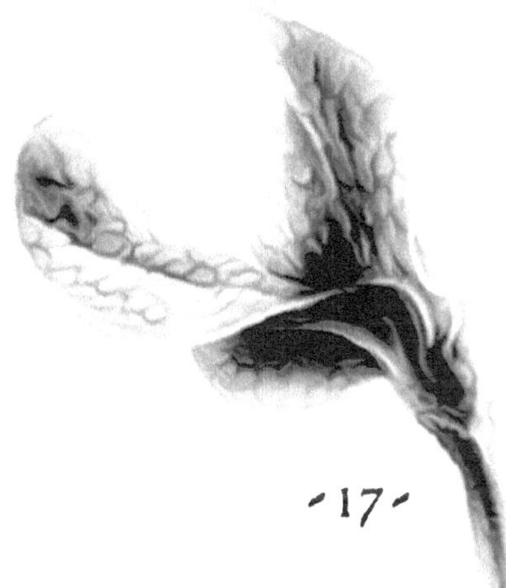

I remember that coolness
that nothingness,
the hours walking the mountain,
the shouts at the summit
and the farewells
that were always so brief,
thinking there would be
seconds and thirds.
The verses I read from the Peruvian Vallejo,
I almost touched the core of my being and held back,
my heart paralyzed with
the scratches from that
cat that didn't want to be saved,
the old loves that filled me
with books and silences.

I remember closing my eyes,
the sky was almost always blue,
I took off my clothes,
filled my mouth with flowers
and my tongue swelled,
I read poems aloud,
waving my fists.

That's how I made love
to my old loves,
with flowers and poems in my mouth,
and the ardor that comes with one who knows
they have nothing else to give:

ardor
  and poetry
    but no future.

Carlota Roby

In the snow
i scratch a poem

In the snow, I scratch a poem,
I dig with my nails
the fallen words.
I see amidst the concrete a flower
that refuses to die,
I think that
        the act of believing is not enough.
In this city,
we emerge like zombies from our
trenches,
we walk to the supermarket
complaining about the cold
with empty hands.
We stop in the middle of avenues
tilting our faces towards the sky,
just as the last cloud dissipates
and a ray of sun touches our skin.
Crows leap
and hide the little light
that remains.
We look at each other at times,
lamenting the lack of euphoria.

Lilith

I sow poems in the ice,
and I think of my grandmother
who never knew snow,
who never learned to write,
who sang from memory poems
by **García Lorca**
believing they were simple songs
from her youth.
Somewhere in the world
the sun burns the skin
of beautiful women who are not
interested in poetry,
they live a carefree life
repeating endlessly
that they're beautiful, young
and happy.
But that's in another part of the world
hcre
is me
writing poems
with the corpses of fallen leaves.

Carlota Roby

In winter a rock is not a rock,
it's a weight around the neck
of a drowned person.

Suddenly,
what was awaited arrives:
       the sound of footsteps
          changes
where there were patches
of grass,
flowers bloom
and the birds sing again.

Then we discover with sadness
that **waiting** is much simpler
than **having**.

Crows leap,
escaping from the light.

**Suddenly it's spring,
and from the damp earth
a poem is born.**

The shapes of Pain

Rock paper scissors,
one two three.
When I showed her my hands
my nanny let out a scream
in the toaster
we only toast the bread
she said, bandaging my hands.

On a bridge near the sea
in a country
I hardly knew,
a girl abruptly stops
in the market;
she looks at me
as if she knows me,
rolls up her skirt and shows me
her scraped knees.

Only angels scrape
only angels burn
        with sweetness.

Carlota Roby

Tell me you're not going to leave,
I wrap my legs
around her waist.

A little Prozac
for laughter.

Here I keep
the lovers
the wounds and
the flowers.

Don't mix
cocaine with
antidepressants.

A girl
points to her
scraped knees,
and I show her my hands,
because I couldn't ask her
in her own tongue
if it hurt.

Proustian memory

I see her on the terrace facing the park
        she wears a yellow hat
                and worn-out jeans.

I can see
the years that have passed
since her last life.
The same gestures:
    **she brings a piece
    of bread to her mouth
    and licks her fingers.**

She speaks
moving her hands
with her thumbs pointing
upwards,
her imperious countenance
like her poetry.

She wears dark glasses,
as always, and a
turtleneck,
severe,
like her.

Carlota Roby

I almost shout your name,
of course you would choose a French breakfast,
like the ones you used to eat
on Sundays before
dancing to songs
in the little theater of Montmartre.

Who were you then?
You watched the moon, and
its omens grew
between your fingers.

For a second she turns around,
takes off her glasses and looks at me,
I eat the madeleine,
take a sip of tea.
Her eyes are not the same,
it's clear it's not you.

Asphalt

**If I say chair
I see
your body seated
crossing one leg over**
the other.

Chin slightly
raised
showing your pride
in life
—and death too—

The rustling leaves of the trees
drown my voice,
the wind in this city
hits my face
even when I close
the windows,
it has overturned your plants
and I've gathered the soil
with my fingers.
Traces of the incense
we burned
last summer.

Carlota Roby

There's an angel
at the door
speaking to me,
resting its wings
over my shadow
telling me it doesn't know how to fly.
My throat chokes,
I wish it were from laughter,
like when they made you
wear false eyelashes
to hunt
ghosts
in that little theater
in Montmartre.
You ran for nothing
in a bad mood
in high heels:
the horror prevails
you declared
with a cigarette in your mouth,
and a Taiwanese film
on the TV.

Lilith

I miss you
always,
on rainy days
jumping over the city's puddles,
throwing stones
at the cars that splashed us
on the sidewalks.

**The sidewalks of this city claim you,
I know they'll be your steps
when the asphalt cracks
and flowers grow from there.**

Carlota Roby

Saint-Jovite

You used to talk about traveling
like an ethereal spirit,
seeing a horizon without end
from the window
of a small house, nestled in the mountains.
Perhaps it was ***Saint-Jovite*** where you envisioned yourself;
we surrounded you on that journey and watched
the machines indicating your heartbeat
and your breath.
It was a tragicomic image
we were there
e x p e c t a n t
as if death
were about to announce herself.
Perhaps we were waiting for her to open
the door of the Intensive Care Unit,
to glance at our shoes as she passed by
to await some esoteric experience.
But death
as we expected
did not come.

Lilith

It only came in other forms,
eyes darkened
fumbling for an exit.
As the poet said:
Where did we expect to find death?
It was right in front of us,
raw and cruel,
a wounded beast,
while we held your hand and told you
 —sometimes lying—
the nurse is coming
and they're going to increase your morphine dosage.

On trees

One cannot
reach a state
prior
to all things:
   returning
   would be not finding,
   and I could no longer see
   my childhood,
   or the two dogs
   that accompanied
   my adolescence;
   nor the cat,
   nor my grandmother's legs
   swaying in the kitchen.

Returning would be to confirm
that everything's been lost:
        the letters,
        the books,
        the painting of that Guajira woman
        kneading dough between her hands;

returning would fill my body with echoes:
         here danced my youth,
         here she made love
         and bid farewell forever to a man
who would have died for her
if she'd asked;
returning would be getting lost
among now unfamiliar mountains,
listing the names
of those who have gone,
forgetting my own,
disappearing a little…
When I was little,
I would take my father's hand
and turn my head upwards
toward the trees.

Now as an adult,
I know we never truly understand
the magnitude of those trees

until
   we see them fall.

If they read that poem
they would know it's me

Carlota Roby

Birds of Lisbon

The curtains float in front
of an open window,
there are white sheets on an empty bed.

The Church of the Three Graces
praying in three bells,
it makes me think of Maria
and her mosaics.

The laughter that comes from the floors
in Alfama.
The drops of water
falling on the ground,
the stone
worn from foot traffic,
wasted like love,
strangers taking photos
on a pink street;
the fleeting smile
of a story that never happens.
The man in love with the birds
soaking his feet
in the sea,
sometimes he turns and looks at me,
as if saying,

Lilith

You have your books
but I have the birds.
He looks like Neptune,
maybe I've imagined it,
but
that autumn afternoon
he owns the sea.

Sitting on the steps
I see the water touch
the old stone;
I think that to return
is to carry on the back
fifty-three moons and a name.

I think of him
when he told me,
It overwhelmed me to see you walk
the same halls from
almost ten years ago.

I think we shared a glance
with some sadness,
because they were the same halls
but not the same steps.

Carlota Roby

And a sense of forgiveness
was born
among us
that took shape
among all the evils
that we caused each other;
and it penetrated the walls
and it let us hear our voices,
and we discovered that they were far away
from another era and from another land,
so old
that it was an obsolete language that we heard.

 And I saw myself again
walking
in front of his balconies
while he read
Beat poetry to me,
which was also his poetry,
because when he wrote he was
O'Hara
and he was Ginsberg
and he was Kerouac
and he was Di Prima

with his cocktail of antidepressants
and his brief stays
in foreign sanatoriums
that never healed him
but made him worse,
and made him write
with more force and more anger
and also, more cruelty;
and he made love to me
dispossessed
of everything
except the idea of me.
And sometimes he repeated my omens
as if they were litanies
canceling the future.
Other times he murmured
prayers to an absent virgin,
the same one that came back
with grenades in her hands
and songs in her mouth
to briefly explain his pain.

Carlota Roby

The sky is so clear
that my feet seem to shine
on the stairs
and I dip my legs
in the water.
The bird man turns
and applauds the sky
celebrating my sudden desire,
my immense courage.
I smile at him and a
loud laughter comes out
of my chest,
and we both laugh
scaring the birds
away.

Carlota Roby

"You and I must have a talk. And
I shiver: let's be brave, shall we?"
Marina Tsvetaeva

Lilith

I

I send you the first verses of **The Rival**,
and I tell you they remind me of you,
especially the word annihilating;
that's the word that comes to my mind
when I think of you
making love to me.
It feels like plummeting
at 400 miles per hour.
Later I learned that of all
the aspects of Lilith,
the one we share
is the rawest,
the most difficult,
the one that promises
nothing but fire,
I can almost taste
the ashes on my tongue.
I am filled with sadness and anger,

Lilith

I push them away,
I attach them to places,
people.
I'm afraid to feel;
I've stifled all those emotions
for so long
that I've packed them like
dynamite in my belly.
I'm a time bomb, can't you see?
I know you can hear it when I breathe.
One day I'll explode,
my chest, wide open
will be a graveyard of released butterflies.
When I say
I want our vampire love,
do you know what I mean?
I want to consume you,
I want us to mock decency,
to set aside innocence
to focus on what's truly urgent:

the truth.

II

In my dreams,
I give birth to monsters.
They're elegant creatures,
resembling *Giacometti* sculptures,
a pair of hands holding the void,
people who seem
to have lost everything.
I think about my dreams,
What is fantasy without reason?
What is love without fear?
Standing before the sculptures,
I think of you
and wonder:
Do we bring out
our subconscious patterns
or do we evoke each other's fears?

Lilith

III

Sometimes I say:
come as you are,
come as my lover
and my executioner.

The door is open.

In my dreams
I tremble,
you beg me to be brave.

Carlota Roby

The Door

You open the door for me
but I refuse to enter.
Instead, I gaze deeply at you
for a long time:
your strong hands hold the door
in the same way
they've held my body
so many times I've lost count,
your clean and polished nails
speak more about you than you think.
You shaved,
though I prefer your two-day stubble.
Thick eyebrows
hiding the unsaid things.
I hate sharing you
with so many other
bodies.
I move my feet in circles:
black high heels
worn by my mother
in the eighties;
left, right, left,
crossing each other,
whispering words in a
foreign language,
I look at the carpet,
I hate postmodernism.

Lilith

I curse you under my breath,
you don't understand what I've said.
Now you seem impatient
I think you might give up
any moment now
but you keep the door open
firmly.
I'm just like you,
instead of turning my back
I keep circling around:
close-up of my feet
–à la Wong Kar-wai–
black high heels dancing;
you can see
clusters of winter berries
growing on them.
I raise my arms,
it could be Christmas Eve,
we could be in New York
where everything always goes so wrong for us.
The hallway is long
and we seem like two abandoned cats,
the chandelier light
casts shadows

Carlota Roby

on your mouth,
I think you're chewing me
but our distance
is irrevocable.
I hear the dripping of a
neighboring faucet,
it brings back
all the fragmentation,
all the hurt:
ten drops,
ten lovers,
ten patterns on the carpet.
We're separated,
but our reflection
is an apparition
in each other's eyes.
We move quietly
like birds of prey
hunting,
I frighten you
and you frighten me.

But your hand
is still there
on the open door,
looking at the things
that look at us,
we mark
the lateness
of our love.
We have chosen
the place of our wound.

You say you're disgusted with astrology
with psychoanalysis
with me.
Where are we going to put the remnants
of this shipwreck when it all ends?

Carlota Roby

The extent of pain

Do you remember the time we saw that woman die,
hit by a car?
She had very long, dark hair; her face
appeared untouched, but she was very pale,
and stems and roots sprouted from her forehead.
Your hands were trembling so much that I had
to grab the steering wheel. You kept repeating,
they killed her, they killed her,
but in reality, we didn't know.

When we got back home, you said you were leaving,
just like that. You packed all your clothes,
unfolded, into two black suitcases,
and I smoked a cigarette without asking you
any questions. You were disoriented,
you took a Valium and two glasses
of wine. And then you sat on the edge
of the stairs and all you did
was cry and tremble for hours. I think
about that and remember my nausea. You mumbled
apologies like rituals and all I could manage
were anemic monosyllables that must have sounded
like a tightrope in the wind.

Lilith

The sun was already beginning to rise when you closed
the door behind you.
You left a scent of cautious flowers
in my nostrils, and then I thought
that the death you had offered me wasn't as final
as the one they gave you. I felt a bit jealous,
not even in the extent of my pain did
I come out as the winner.

Carlota Roby

A Dead and a Ritual

My Lilith is here
holding her candles
in each eyelid
she carries
a dead and a ritual.
She asks them to come back
and cuts her hands
over an improvised sanctuary.

Lilith
who did nothing but fight
for her life,
gives it all away
and lays down to die
among the firewood.
She is flanked,
protected by whores,
          s n i p e r s
                    and poets.

Vultures on the Roof

You speak of vultures on the roof
and show me a photo of the skylight
of your house. You say they perch there,
gazing down at you, and sometimes you think
the bars will collapse
and the large birds will swoop down
upon your head. I tell you they would
spread their wings and fly far away to avoid falling.
You think otherwise,
and say their own weight would bring them crashing down.
We look at each other, and I wonder
if I'm the vulture falling upon your head, or the
head receiving the impact.
The sun shines and I see droplets of sweat
on your forehead
glistening like frost.
I look at you, with the same attention
with which I feel you
go silent on the phone.

Carlota Roby

I touch your forehead, trace my finger
around your eyes, bring it
to the tip of my tongue and taste
your entire body in that gesture.
I taste your body and all the
bodies you've tasted.
I taste your finger and
we somersault
on the sand of some country
forgotten by our enemies.
I open my eyes
and you speak of vultures on the roof
and I know that
something will separate
me from you
if I stay,
and something of me
                    will always remain
                        with you if I go.

A fly violently crushed
on the pavement
reminded me
of the way we used to love

Carlota Roby

You call me with a fever
and i crush a paper bag
against the receiver

Not everyone can handle the power,
you said, holding in your hands
a broken gas mask
on an embankment.
You looked like a rebellion
of sad faces.

Kneeling down,
you apologized to the birds.

I knelt beside you and we smoked
in silence,
aware that nothing
in life repeats itself the same;
never again,
you and me,
with a broken gas mask
at our feet,
while the birds flew
accepting apologies.

Lilith

Never again,
will we kneel like that,
waving our arms against the wind
aware of time
and its knives.

Sometime,
perhaps
someone else,
but not us,
nor the wind,
nor the fly you crushed
against the pavement
with mechanical fury,
looking into my eyes
imagining my entire body
contained in its guts.

There are poems that come out in one shot
and there are others that cannot be saved.

Love is the same.

Carlota Roby

Seven requiems and a love

"At the end of my suffering, there was a door."
Louise Glück

I

When the end comes
we don't
realize it.
Before that
we make a lot of noise
to pretend control.
I told you this
twice
and you laughed,
placing your glass
on the marble.
That's what you usually do
when you get nervous:
you drink a little,
tell stupid jokes
and bite your skin.

II

Your back rests
on the windowsill.
I store you in my head
like a verse by Louise
in my diary.
Suddenly,
time looms
over us
and I know that one afternoon I'll be
remembering this day
when your index finger
touched my knee,
and a ray of sunlight pierced
the brief space
between our lips.
That day I saw you dangling your legs
off the couch
and I thought you were a child
scared in the dark.
I wonder if you also
saw the scared girl
sitting in front of you.
Each with their own cruelty
only a part of it revealed.

III

I see you walk away in hurried steps.
It makes sense, I think.
You couldn't change who you are.
You couldn't even change
the simplest facts.

IV

Fool,
you thought you could
appease the beasts.
What were you counting on?
On some tricks
and pathologies diagnosed
by questionable doctors.
Many attempts
for lack of character
or audacity.
Sometimes
Xanax,
others,
marijuana,
always poetry.

V

Idiot,
now you see that some things happen
and don't come back.
For example, I'll never again
experience what it feels like
to watch a Bergman or Tarkovsky film
for the first time,
and you
will never again feel what it's like
to see me in the background
sitting with a glass
waiting for you.

VI

The days of your love
were
the lights
of a waiting room.
For days
my poems covered
its bare corners,
and one afternoon without thinking
windows appeared open
in my hands.

VII

No one tells us
what to do
at the end of our
great loves.

Carlota Roby

POV

As everything else passed,
so did the fear
of external forces
pouncing upon me.
Could I have escaped?
Sometimes surrender
is the only
dignified action;
knowing how to die
is hard,
I won't deny it;
more than flying
and shivering
against the windows,
dying takes work,
and there lies the only
truth.

Lilith

Once
I loved
among figs
and other fruits,
violence always
waved its fingers,
I couldn't conceive life
without an escape;
love was brief
my pleasures too,
unlike you
I didn't need matter,
I saw the light for what it was;
why should I explain everything
that existed in the world,
why not let it be;
I roamed through fields,
sailed through different ages and times,
I didn't have the constraints of time,
only my freedom
and unlike you
I never feared her.

Veils of tulle

I dream that I have died
and an old love appears
at my grave.
He brings veils of tulle
over his eyelids,
murmurs my name,
pausing his tongue at
the second syllable.
He speaks to me slowly
as I once spoke to him.
Then his voice transforms
upon exhaling and contains
all of the voices of the future.
He says he has finally
forgiven me:
    there are no more old ghosts
    on the stairs,
    or secret codes
    in the photographs,
    only the inexorable reality
    of winter
    in its coldest nights.

Lilith

Sometimes he misses
the way my head
spawned roots
and ascended to the ceiling.
He says that one day he believed
that I was the origin of all
things,
but that was a mistake.
He masturbates
while reading the poems
we didn't believe ourselves
capable of writing,
and then he bids farewell.

Carlota Roby

The red bricks

I see marks of fallen leaves
on the asphalt.
This is how
I'll remember you
as the years pass by.
A flock of birds
come from the future
to tell me that love
is not being able to express
the other's sadness.

I hope your life
is sweet
like the fruits we
ate in the south;
may your mornings fill
with brightness
over all your darkness,
and may you learn to hold
your breath in the lakes
when the beasts arrive.

Lilith

Over the mirror,
my eyes
that were once yours
in the city of
red bricks.

Listen, there's no love
         without punishment,
         nor is there oblivion
that doesn't contain the origin
of fear.

Carlota Roby

The unburdening

I want to say your name
but when I do
I kill you,
and I'm already naming
someone else.
There are certain wills
that merit
an unburdening.
I ask if you understand
what I'm saying,
but you keep silent,
hypnotized
by the violence my words carry:
obscene words
spoken softly,
with the sweet tone
that things have
when they are born.

Lilith

To unburden,
to disconnect
to separate
deliberately
the burdens of a system
to preserve its integrity.
To eliminate burdens,
I tell you,
for the common good.
You don't like how it sounds,
it smells like communism,
like sacrifice.
To separate
like saying goodbye,
like returning
to the place you didn't dare
to leave.
You take a photo of me,
I misquote Schopenhauer
but you believe me,

you say nothing when
I quote him again and speak
in the third person
of the plural,
as if Arthur and I
were one entity:
we believe that
to die should be considered
the true aim of life.
You look at my body
naked in front of the mirror.
We spend half an hour
trying to emulate a scene
from **Béla Tarr**,
we give up
when the clock strikes two.
Happiness is incidental,
I tell you,
our only option is to suffer less.
We make love
and for a few minutes
we believe the argument is closed;
we hear the sound of drops falling
from the roof.

Lilith

We are at the point
where we abbreviate
our names,
because names
always seem
too long
at the beginning of love,
as if pronouncing them in full
were a waste,
as if we risked
losing it.

WANTED:
LOST LOVE
IN THE SECOND SYLLABLE.

You close the curtains,
love has no space to escape,
    not through your mouth,
not through mine,
not through the cracks in the walls;
not through the open windows,
not through the drops that plummet
and fall with brief sighs

Carlota Roby

while you look at your phone
and I underline
a verse
in the poetry book
I found
on a street
where we floated over
jacarandas
that when touched
sounded like a mellotron.
One day we'll be fed up
with the rites
of the idiotic semantics
we settle for
to seem
more or less digestible.
But you and I know better:

we are in search
of a language
that allows us to explain
the highest metaphysical truths.
You kiss my feet,
I bite your mouth
you write me a handwritten letter
and bid farewell saying
believe in my good feelings.
One day I will want to remember
that I was here
biting your lips
thinking about how
the sun's rays pierced
your eyes
illuminating my fears.

Carlota Roby

The lovers

I

She sat
in front of the window
wanting to stay there
in the void
where nothing was past yet.
Who said
waiting made her patient;
who said she wasn't
full of rage?
Now you see her silhouette
raising her arm,
as if demanding a payment.
What do you owe her?

You kiss me
then straighten your shirt
carefully.

II

You tried to explain
as best you could
with brief and assuring words
to calm her horror.
And I whispered in your ear
(which was also hers)
I can't live to comfort you,
and it was there when they sealed
all the mirrors,
but of course
there remained
the thread figurines
in your pockets,
the bloodied soldiers
in the folds of your boots,
and my hands on your face
like a still from *Rossellini*
in black and white.

III

A bomb
that failed to
explode
is now safely hidden.

IV

Sometimes I imagine you standing in the kitchen
dismissing comments,
demanding nuances,
you probably say something like:
Well,
all you had to do
was ask.

Lilith

V

The story is wrongly told,
it wasn't the Nymph who stopped
the hero from leaving,
it was he who insisted to stay.

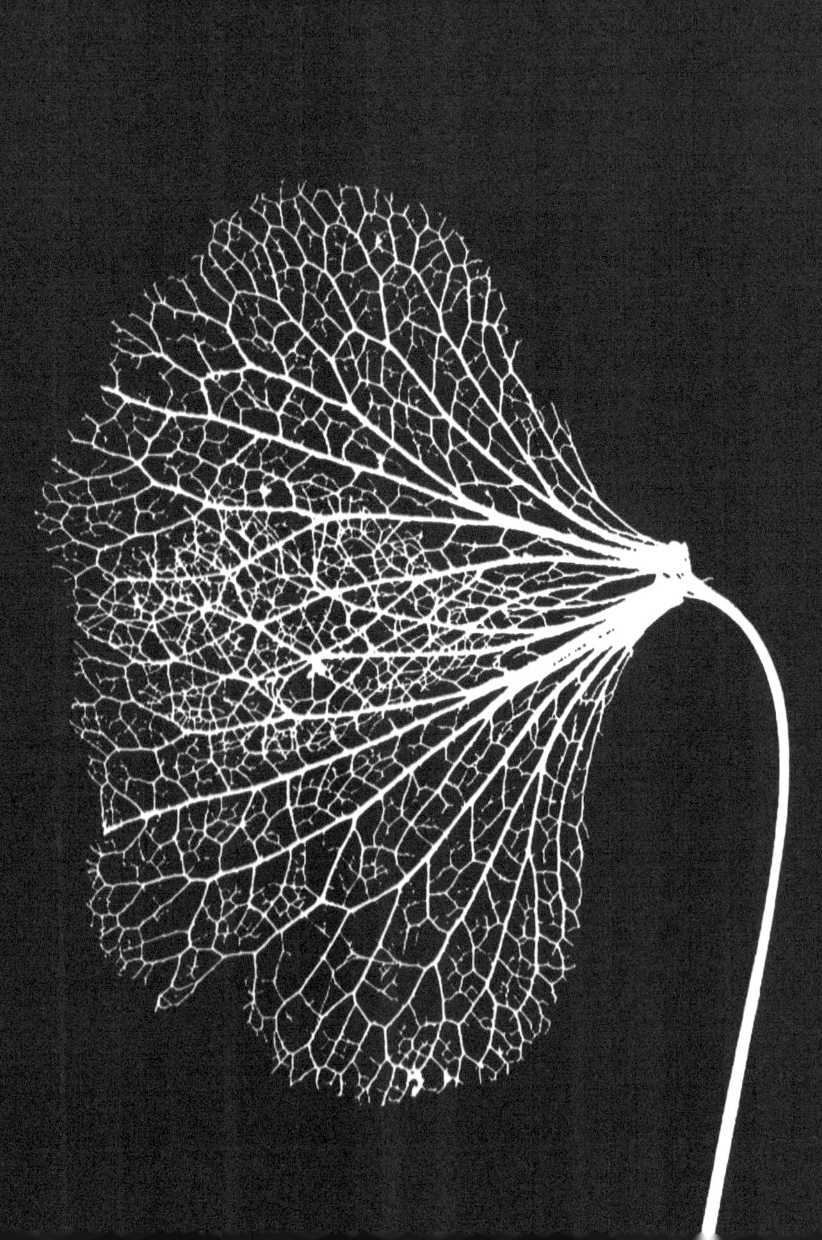

Your eyes
windows of open
corpses.

I turn my back on a love

On the windowsill
a wounded bird perches,
we recognize each other
but when I try to approach
it dives down
simulating a suicide.

It's a night of eclipses,
I cross the street
and something is ending,
I think I know what it is,
on the pavement
I see the dead bird
in its rigor mortis,
I see an omen,
and I foolishly think
that I could escape
from the void to which this compulsion
to love has brought me.
But there's a hand that ignores
the sharpness of the knife,
a tongue
seeking to quench its thirst.

Have you turned your back on
a love?

Lilith

What will you do when
it's your turn in the trial,
and the moment has come to
confront the god
you so vehemently deny?
Will you enumerate your victims?
Will you justify your actions with your fear?

I will say
that mercy must always be
the guiding principle of the one
who rules the realms and opens the doors
to eternity.

But God,
your forgiveness doesn't concern me,
eternity is just
another whim;
I want to be cosmic dust,
regenerate from mourning
never returning;
I want poppies to bloom in
the fields
and mirrors in the clearings
to show me all the angles
from where the sun sets,
tongues of fire

Carlota Roby

to appear in the cracks
of my empty belly,
the subliminal creation of a scream
to soothe the burning of youth
which inevitably comes to an end.

God,
you never speak of the number of
men you sacrificed
crafting walled deceptions
with tall walls of cement
and blood.
If you don't want to speak of sacrifices,
then tell me,
How many have I saved
in the place where the horizon ends
and the sun dies?

Who will count all that I was?
In whose hands will end
my bruised ego,
my convulsions
my insatiable thirst?

Lilith

When this burning ends,
will all my geologies end too?
I lack the beauty of the moon,
my thought chose its own
form,
it has decided
to straighten the falling tree,
not to be the tree

Beauty!
When has that complacent villainess
ever saved me?
Violent
and uncomfortable,
truth has saved me!

Carlota Roby

Spider woman

In a corner
the spider woman
submits her sex
to discussion.

Behold the triangle
of fire,
the starched bags
of obscene souls.

Two golden coins
make noise as they fall,
and the spider woman lifts
her gaze.

Tonight
she doesn't want to stir
certain ideas,
only to create the void,
which is to say

to create the place where
the body of all
lovers
no longer hesitates
and jumps into the void
in a perfect state
of convulsion.

Artaud!

Two bodies crash
against the asphalt,
their bones sound
like golden coins
falling to the ground.

The spider woman
collects her memories,
jealously
in a corner.
The night is still possible,
as a multitude awaits her
in the hallway.

Carlota Roby

Her old versions
and the new ones,
those that have not yet formed,
and those that have dissolved.

In the distance she sees a lost bird;
she recognizes it by the carnation
it carries in its beak.
The bird advances
and the asphalt creaks.

All her versions
chant the name
of the bird,
that is,
the name of whomever
the bird once was,
because how to name it,
how
with just one mouth?

Lilith

The spider woman
submits her past to discussion
but does not speak of the future,
because the future
is yet to come,
and by this I mean
it never arrives.

The coins

I

We sit by the lake
dipping our feet in the water.
I wiggle my toes,
and a man I recognize from my childhood
o b s e r v e s   m e
and then does the same.

How can I give you what you don't have?
The courage,
the blackberries,
the fig trees.
Let go of anger,
you've always liked revenge.
I laugh:
I'll take my anger to the lake
and I'll still be left with the lake.

Lilith

At this point
he says,
*I've come to confuse
certain parts
of my life
and in some chapters,
you even acquire
good qualities.*

**I open my pocket
and give him a coin.**
I'll pay your fare.
**There's no fear in his hands
just denial.**

II

Pay your debts,
you tell me
as you get up.

The coins fall to the ground
loudly
they tremble
like bombs.

I have no debts
(I ignore it).

You said,
hold my hand tightly,
but it was you
who couldn't keep the pace.

Now the coins float
like particles of skin
pierced by a ray of sun.

On the bathroom wall
among vinyl records,
I saw a poem by **Mir**.

Later, I told you
**There's a country
in the world.**

You didn't understand what I meant.

Eden was
far away from us,
it all seemed
so boring too.

I think you're a good man.

Let me rephrase:

I think you try
to be a good man
and the effort is, at least,
commendable.

The coins fall to the ground,
my upper lip trembles.
You always managed to disguise
your simplicities.

Lying is simple,
it's the truth that
requires much more
from us.

Carlota Roby

Carousels and vertigo

Cold spheres
over cold hands
reading a universal
treatise,
or testaments of
birds hopping on the sidewalks.
It's autumn
and the sun still warms enough
to think that cold won't come.
Flowers stand tall like Venus
rising from a deep sleep
and you and I
with wild amazement
ask for forgiveness.
Always silent,
failing inexorably.
Carousels and vertigo
on the pavement.
There's a fire
resting in my chest,
while your heart sounds
like an intensive care unit.

Lilith

I only believe
in shadows and music.
There's a melody playing
from a balcony:
I want to create something
that doesn't involve
an explosion.
To write, for example,
about the dry roots
of a fallen tree,
or the open eyelids
of a dead person.
**A poem that speaks of
the impossibility of joy.**

Carlota Roby

This is not a prayer,
much less
a hope.

Language persists
like the remnants of a love,
like the whispers of my grandmother
in the chapel,
like leaves falling
unwilling to make noise,
almost with a sorrow for dying.
There are lost rows
in my memory
of a time
of late resistance.
I was once there
in that country
of dead men and poets.
It wasn't the accent,
nor the colors,
but something of its sadness
that must have remained in me.
The dried chrysanthemums
on the ceiling
look perplexed
at how obscene
forgetfulness appears from there.

Lilith

She doesn't know how to scream
but she knows how to hurt.
Each chrysanthemum is
a violent form
of love.
Ancient cathedrals
in the distance,
full of omens.
All my devotion
turned into violence.

Close the windows,
these are not hours
to cry.

One night I saw him in the distance,
his forehead falling onto the dust,
I tried to tell him that
when the end of the world comes
he should hang
from the stars,
or at least
from the requiem
of a love.

But it was a lie,
if the end of the world comes
not even language
will make sense.
He seemed to hear me
because he began
to meow at the cats
and they, naturally,
answered him.

That was a while ago,
when we still believed
nuclear disarmament was possible,
when we read **Kawabata**
and enchantments sprang from my hands.

There's a crack
in all things,
but I want
to break him myself.

Lilith

To exercise hope,
I sit in front
of the window for hours
thinking that now
I'm going to lose my mind,
but night comes
and I don't lose it.

One day I'll be
like **Connie Converse,**
and I hope they'll say
that I loved intensely
and then
they never saw me again.

I no longer wonder
where you are

Moonlight

> *"Poet, what worries you*
> *has nothing to do with the moon."*
> **Antonin Artaud**

In my dreams, I am sitting on the edge of the world,
the full moon shines upon my shoulders
and I think that maybe for a minute or two
life is possible.

I hear it:
I was born as many and died as one.

I chase my versions across the lake,
and the ones that I were and the ones I hope to be
are the same
from which I will escape one day,
as I did with all the others.

Carlota Roby

I shout at them
How dare you disappear like that?
And suddenly you appear
as if my plea were
some kind of enchantment,
a spell hard to break.

You appear and bring fish in your hands,
as an offering,
you place them at my feet.
You pick my doubts at random,
you deposit them on the sand
like murky secrets you don't want
to carry.
You enjoy seeing me undress
and enter the water
repeating my desires quietly,
you don't believe in the moon as I do
and that may be your problem,
you don't believe in anything omnipresent
except yourself.
I swim underwater
and see fluorescent fish,
they show me the change of course

that the future will take
reading the leaves of the algae,
certain eventualities
that will change my plans.
I'm afraid of oblivion
I tell them,
and I come out to breathe,
my head illuminated,
a lunatic and atmospheric coronation.
I look for you,
it smells of salt and you're already gone.
I think I've attributed to you
extraordinary qualities
you don't have,
that is,
I've made you seem much more interesting
in my poems;
you know I'm prone to endless fictions.
A cloud covers the moon
and we are left in the dark,
the lake, the fish, and I:

I hear your footsteps in the sand.

Carlota Roby

I'm not afraid anymore

There are no quiet corners in the house,
the windows are open
and the beasts have entered.
They are sweet beasts, with deep eyes
that let me massage their drooping eyelids.
I keep my hands in my pockets.

I want to pierce through my own myths,
shatter the glass in my hands,
now that the nodes have changed,
now that I know the ritual of stripping
like **Inanna**,
I shed the layers, and I arrive
backwards into the deepest darkness.

This house is a cradle
and a tomb,
a **l u l l a b y**
and a requiem.

Lilith

Silence,
the beasts command me,
they say the paths of the underworld
are perfect,
and I must not question them.
Poor soft barbarians,
they think one day they will see love
and they'll be able to survive it.

They repeat that I'm a mortal
wandering the corridors,
they point at me with their open claws,
they think they will never die.

Little fools,
dying is difficult,
dying takes work
and the dead that remain
will be mine.

What was missing?
A father, a mother,
I was also missing
twisting naked
in front of the mirror
at the precise moment
you turn on
the light.

I whisper
sacred songs
to you
in a language you don't understand.

I'm
  not
    afraid
       anymore.

Carlota Roby

Shadows

I

There is a shadow at the edge of the lake.
Slowly she lowers her hands and joins them
in the water, measuring the void.
It's long like her fingers
as they elongate into the darkness.
Barefoot, I walk slowly
listening to the leaves crunch
beneath my weight.
Distances are long
when silence is long.

Lilith

II

There was a time when I thought
that everything was possible,
from the most beautiful
to the most atrocious.
I imagined houses with high ceilings
and they appeared when I opened my eyes;
I imagined torture chambers
and I heard the screams.
There was a time I ran
through fields more remote than this,
with the sharp laughter of childhood
cutting my throat.

III

I know the smell of your embraces
and the universe hidden
in your scraped knees
harmed by wicked angels.
Don't tell me that life passes,
don't speak to me of time
and its punishments.

IV

From the cicadas
I learned a language;
in my ears they whispered
omens
that encircled
my mortality.

V

Now infinite mirrors are what I find.
All my versions
lull their shadows to sleep
with whispers and chants.
At their feet, I forge a poem,
at their feet, I place the first
and last full moon.

VI

There is a life, ***I shout to them,***
that, had we known,
we would have chosen.
They turn their vague faces,
and though they have no eyes
their gazes suffocate me:
> ***it's not sadness that I see,***
> ***it's something much worse.***

Carlota Roby

The sad notebooks

There's a drop descending on the trunk
of a willow. There's a coppery world
that one can glimpse within.
M o l e c u l e s
of birds, atoms of the sun,
tiny fragments of skin
from people who have departed.

The drop falls,
first slowly, then suddenly,
as if escaping some possibility.
There's a drop descending on the trunk
of the tree that saw me grow.
I see it, with my chin
resting on the windowsill.
I've returned to the origin of all things,
to the place I swore not to return.

The willow remains there, watching
the drops that pass down its trunk
like invalid insects
dead from the cold.

Lilith

Night falls, and it unleashes
the beasts
that rule this empty house,
their steps echoing from the basement.
Here, God is a twisted pipe.

Somewhere in these corners
lay my sad notebooks,
with their ardors and their nostalgias;
their sips of dirty water and pillboxes;
their fierce resistance, their precipices.
But I don't open the drawers,
I let the moths rest,
gnawing memories in my hands.

Suddenly the music
that no longer plays;
daguerreotypes of another life,
where it was easy to say I wanted to die
because I knew nothing of pain,
nor the passage of time
and all that it takes away.

Candle marks, and worms:
there was an entire life here,
here lies the life that could have been.

Carlota Roby

Oath

A cat walks upon my shadow
and declares it as its own.
There is no violence in its conquest;
nor is there kindness.
As soon as I resist,
it will claw my eyes out.

The shadow is there,
amplified
by the light filtering in
from ancient cathedrals.

**City of catacombs
and corpses.**

Like your memory in my mind,
full of invented
conversations
where I improve
our rhetoric
and our capacity
t o   h a t e .

I know it is useless
to invoke other bodies,
while I make love
in the mornings.
Or to invoke other endings
for my sad poems
that always speak of you.

I could talk about this
or other things,
become a soluble
substance
in a sudden gesture
of maturity and simplicity.

Talk, for example,
about the way **Fito** waves his hands;
about the fortified cities
in the Caribbean,
or the force of the ocean
against those walls.

I could talk about the country
of dead poets,
or of a fictional homeland
where it doesn't smell of oblivion;
or more simply,
about the roots of trees
breaking through
blocks of concrete.

Fierce force
that reclaims spaces
that were once its own.

Perhaps
-someday-
in my homeland too,
trees with stubborn roots.

Brute
Force

like what my body
demands of you
in front of the windows.

Lilith

Poison
Poison

I don't want anymore.

Singing into the void,
towards the place
where my voice becomes
a soluble substance
that you consume,
from my body to your throat
you end up mute
with vertigo,
of an emptiness that is yours
here in the center of my belly.

Hostile
Hostile

like vultures
on the imaginary roofs
that I construct in your mouth.

Carlota Roby

I don't want anymore
I don't want anymore

except to explain
that it's useless
to have loved so much.

**It serves no purpose,
I swear.**

Once I wanted to be something else:
a poisonous mushroom,
a gunshot,
the word that would end
an important sentence.

Carlota Roby

Wet grass

Alejandra said that a glance from the sewer could be a vision of the world. My friend Ceci says it's not true, but she had the luck of growing up reading Dostoevsky. The lavenders push up through the earth with that audacity that beings have when they are born. A woman scares flies away with her hands. In spring, everything seems possible, even you, but when I told you this, you looked at me and I knew you hadn't understood. This is not a garden, I told you sitting on the wet grass,

it is poetry

The storm

That night we sensed
the smell of the storm
from afar,
it smelled like verdigris
and burnt cinnamon.
We ran out of the woods.
You fell and scraped your left knee,
and when we cleaned the wound,
we saw the silhouette of the Virgin Mary
in your scar.

We laughed about it,
    yet we lit a candle
            just to be sure.

The cracks

I

Every day beneath the stairs
   I see a black cat that doesn't exist
      on stairs that don't exist
         that hold the steps of a woman
            who doesn't exist.

II

It was an abandoned house in Lansing, Michigan. We talked about the weather and airplanes. That conversation yielded nothing but vague observations that may or may not fit into a pattern I didn't perceive. She said, **"This house belongs to the bird that has built a nest in each of its rooms."** But this was met with misunderstanding. I remember kissing her beneath the fig tree. She laughed and squeezed my hands under the table.

Lilith

III

It seems to me that sometimes, when I look into your eyes, I see a river. A river I remember from my childhood. The lights were so dim that we could barely see things as they were. I imagined a lit fireplace and curtains billowing as the wind struck the windows. Who are we to ask for more if we possess the fire? And I tell you that I always imagine other worlds, sometimes not even better, but at least different from this one. A world that doesn't crush me into nothingness: a beautiful experiment. We fell silent, and I saw the past dancing in the living room.

What are you feeling?
Do you feel anything?
And I think you smiled.

IV

You will become what we wanted you to be:
        over-civilized
        over-developed
        over-abandoned.
        And sometimes we would think
        about how the years to come would be:
          the years of *happy hours*
            and happy families.

V

This is the place
where our bodies
were buried
among rituals and praises.
I remember our ridiculous
golden suits
and the glitter on the ground.

VI

I don't think it means much
to have an open window
if we're afraid to fly.
Tell me,
where will our old versions dwell?
Winning is worthless
if we fail them.

VII

I hope we know how to suffer as we have loved. At the
origin of all things that fear cracks. I believe in the cracks:
legs open in front of the mirror showing us the origin of
the world. There goes our love, swelling like a drowned
man, and our hands mimicking the flight of a bird. May
our sadness be brief. May those we have wanted to be, be
who we are.

VIII

From you
like from the south
I demand it all.

Workshop for mending deflated tires

I remember the prayers
we learned as girls
the psalms
the proverbs
the sacrifices,
the glitter sprinkling our
faces
that the most devout mistook
for miracles,
the crosses on the roads
"here died a name"
the immense basilicas filled with
white virgins,
the scandals of good girls,
the secrets
the revenges
ink-written in
the bathrooms.
We lived in the confessionals,
always penitents
surrounded by white saints;
men of questionable virtues
who opened metamorphic spaces
in their tales of dissected ***Lolitas***.

Carlota Roby

We were too intelligent
for their brief machinations,
their cheap politics of the body.

But those were ancient nights
where the greatest sacrifice
was to nod and be silent;
we wanted to do good
while touching our bodies,
the changing rooms
before volleyball or gymnastics,
a good education that consisted of
coming to terms with ourselves,
in accepting a life
(more or less mediocre)
with anyone capable
of changing a tire,
or opening a jar of
jam in the mornings.
A man of good education and
principles,
who knew how to lie
the way those who agree
to a life more or less mediocre
must lie,
and cover up their affairs in the
refrigerator.

Lilith

We were so young
that the drums of the great
revolutions sounded in the distance,
and we called them ours
because we were
heiresses of an absolute and feverish
future,
the ideas and desires were ours,
the deaths of the birds,
the bitter bursts of innocence,
the bundle of legs,
the nights and the lakes,
the secret kisses,
everything was ours.
The future looked at us
and we followed its orders,
kneeling
on the marble,
sinking our fangs
into the bread
which were flesh and omen on
our tongues
which already ventured into other
corners.

*It's worrisome not to be able to see what's
coming*
we heard adults say,
while drinking liquor after
dinner,
and fantasizing about the loves
of their youth,
in constant mourning, always.

So we took turns watching
from the window,
waiting for a tsunami,
an ancestral sphere
full of lights,
or some satellite to tell us
firsthand
what was coming.

At night,
we captured the future
between glass,
our dreams kneeling
in the sand.
And on a night of eclipse,

Lilith

a battalion of seagulls
sealed the sky with
shadows over a full moon;
we detached
from windows that,
as girls
we watched with diligence,
and began to think about
ourselves
like those seagulls that caught
the sky,
only to abandon it later,

**muted screams
and then,
a profound silence.**

Carlota Roby

The offering

To touch the abstract core
of eclipses and storms,
spreading in your hands
pieces of infinity.
W o m a n, destroyer of taboos,
you rise to the sky
and play a harp
that you've built on the earth
of myths.
You open your hands
and release
all the birds of the world.

Leucadia

To the North of Ithaca, your body occupied its final space
not even poetry could save you
from the absence of love.
Your last verse, a scream,
resonates in the ravines of the Ionian Sea.

Sleep now,
the birds will not forget your name,
the goddess and her sparrows will gather
your body from the waves.

Invoke her now,
she shall save you
with immortal lips
when your
       ultimate
        darkness
          arrives.

Carlota Roby

Vestals

They starve
the priestess,
then bury
her body
and her poems,
whispering vows
over broken windows
in their enchantments,
they spell out
the rites;

they bind the hands
that could not hold
the sacred flames.
The gift has been
denied to her,
the language
on its shores holds
two secrets.

Hunger
to kill
a woman's body.

Lilith

To kill
  and then
    to found
      a city
        where laws,
          obedience
            and flowers
              can grow.

Carlota Roby

Allegory of the earth

She implores to the sky
with her hands
over her head,
as if only the sky
could save her
from this compulsion.
There are demons that
change shape;
there are angels too.
She knows she can give
space to all,
the similarity between her body
and the vast universe
causes poppies to grow
on her fingers.
She doesn't smile,
she sits stunned
with an implausible gesture
towards the vast life
that opens before her.

Lilith

She tastes fistfuls of earth
savoring the hidden
past that precedes her.
Eyes of a wounded deer,
fabricating within her veins
the great insurrection.

Little else interests her
she only wants to be the flower
that holds the hand
of a dead person.
Eternity
is a valley
full of bodies
entombed
by ancient
explosions.

Books speak little
about it,
it's a certainty
among poets
who approach the precipice
to free themselves from their immortality.

Carlota Roby

Allegory of fire

Cerberus awaits
at the border
which you cross backward
with a flower in hand.
It was of no use for you to fight
against the might of a god
who left your thighs
marked with
the strength of his love;

or so he called it,
when he showed you
      the night
      under the shadowy
      lush
      of his rages.

A double promise
from where heads of serpents are born.
You will be the ruler of an empire,
a widow facing an open grave.
You imagine stealing the divine powers
from the god who deceived you,
and you yourself choose the golden crown.

Lilith

In vain does he try to understand
the mysteries that occupy you.
You have abandoned hope
and thus too,
f e a r .

Now you recount briefly
the journey you undertook
from the center of the earth.

You seek his eyes
among the obscene people
as you cross the river
stepping on the drowned.

These are your dominions,
with authority
you preside over them.

You dance the dance
                of war,
you taste the power and
keep it.

Carlota Roby

You are compassionate towards
the heroes
for you sense the same traces
of foolish passion
that you see in his pupils.

You order that your name
shall not be spoken
except by those initiated
in your rites.

Why be the goddess
of flowers
if you can be
the one who decides
when winter arrives?

State of siege

We've spoken words,
enchantments that awaken
the fury from their graves,
prophecies
of sweet gas
and euphoria.

We've died
for you,
for the flowers
that bloom
in the ocean,
drowned
or thirsty,
thrown away
stoned,
vanished.

We've ruled
a nation,
spread its wings;
we no longer remember
if it's Mesopotamia,
Constantinople,
Egypt
or Eden

What does it matter!
If a new life arises

Dark
   m a g i c

neither decency
nor mercy,
nor contracts
nor barter,
nor kitchens;
we rise
and we are rock
ground
ashes
bone,
and with our hands
we make man
and give him a sunset;

we are earth
and figs,

they throw stones at us,
we open our coat
they call us witches,
we stick out our tongues.

Lilith

We arrive with whip and diligence,
we taste power on our lips:
we keep it.
We show you our fangs
the daggers
the castle

in the dungeons:
lovers
and enemies.

We kneel
only before cats
give us vertigo,
feed
the birds

d a rk
  m a g i c

we are
disappointed
by your manipulative
practices;

you took our language
and our gestures,
you besieged our cities
but the moon shines
and we pirouette
in a country
forgotten by
our enemies.

Eden is far away
(also so boring).
How many mirrors
have we lived in?

An army accepts defeat
with grace,
between trances and ruins
we rise
and we make man
and give him fire
and deliver a civilization
into his hands.

But it's on us
where language shines,
where the seas bleed
the fire goes out.

    May flowers grow
          where there were ashes.

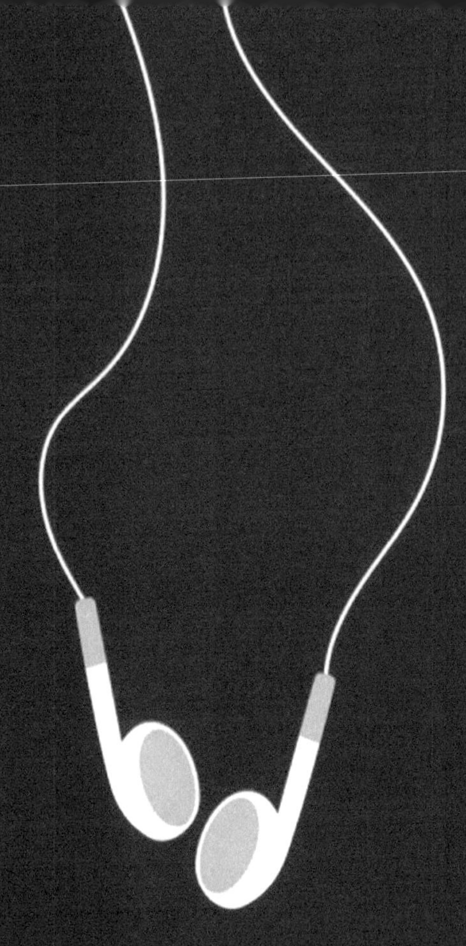

playlist

charlas verticales ♡
by Vocales Verticales

1:11　　　　　　3:31

Carlota Roby

Born in Venezuela, Carlota Roby is a poet who resides in Washington D.C.

About Vocales Verticales

Vocales Verticales is a collaborative project founded by Angie Roby and Carlota Roby, dedicated to cultivating inclusive spaces, both online and in-person, for people who share a passion for poetry, literature, and the arts. Our mission is to make these enriching experiences accessible to everyone and thus foster connections. We believe in the democratic nature of poetry and the arts, and we advocate for their universal enjoyment.

Instagram: @VocalesVerticales
Substack: **Vocales Verticales Substack**
Spotify: **Charlas Verticales**
Youtube: **Vocales Verticales**

TIN
TA
PU
JO

INDEX

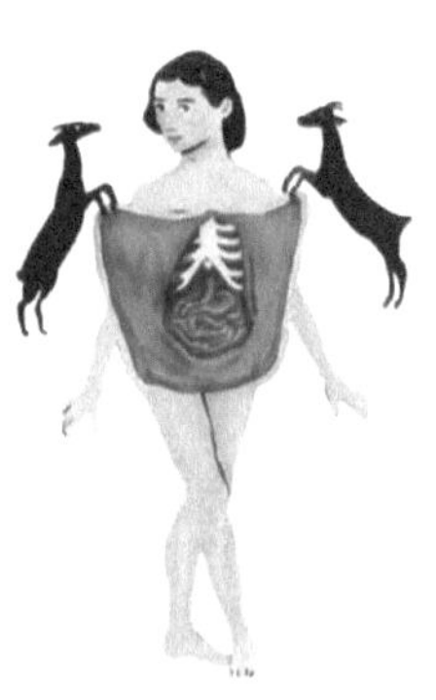

9 789566 315254